NOT YOUR NEST!

by **GIDEON STERER**

illustrated by **ANDREA TSURUMI**

Dial Books
for Young Readers

For C.C. and Abba and Mom —G.S.

To Joan Fenrow —A.T.

Dial Books for Young Readers

Penguin Young Readers Group

An imprint of Penguin Random House LLC

375 Hudson Street

New York, NY 10014

Printed in China
ISBN 9780735228276

10 9 8 7 6 5 4 3 2 1

Design by Jennifer Kelly
Text set in TsurumiFont3

The artwork for this book was inked with pencil and colored digitally.